Monster Mayhem

by **Katie Dale**
illustrated by **Dean Gray**

"Sleep well, little monsters," said Mum.

"Do not let the bed bugs bite!"

said Dad.

"I cannot sleep," said little Sniff.

"What if the bed bugs bite me?"

"I will frighten them off!" said Wiff.

"For I am the most scary monster of all."

"I will frighten off the bed bugs

with my horrid monster SMELL!"

"You do stink," said Tiff.

"But I am the most scary monster of all."

"For I will frighten off the bed bugs
with my sharp monster NAILS!"

"You do have the sharpest nails,"

said Biff.

"But I am the most scary monster
of all."

"For I will frighten off the bed bugs with my big monster TEETH!"

"But I am the most scary monster
of all."

"For I have the biggest roar!"

"I will frighten off the bed bugs
with my big monster..."

The little monsters ran back into bed.

27

"Mum will frighten off the bed bugs," said Biff.

"She is the most scary monster!" said Wiff.

They all agreed.

Quiz

1. Why can't Sniff sleep?
a) Bed bugs might bite him
b) Monsters might scare him
c) It's too dark

2. How would Wiff scare the bed bugs?
a) With his hair
b) With his horns
c) With his smell

3. How would Biff scare the bed bugs?
a) With his hands
b) With his teeth
c) With his eyes

4. What does the monsters' mum shout?
a) BOO!
b) WAA!
c) ROAR!

5. Who is the most scary monster?
a) Sniff
b) Mum
c) Griff

Turn over for answers

Book Bands for Guided Reading

The Institute of Education book banding system is a scale of colours that reflects the various levels of reading difficulty. The bands are assigned by taking into account the content, the language style, the layout and phonics. Word, phrase and sentence level work is also taken into consideration.

Maverick Early Readers are a bright, attractive range of books covering the pink to white bands. All of these books have been book banded for guided reading to the industry standard and edited by a leading educational consultant.

Pink
Red
Yellow
Blue
Green
Orange
Turquoise
Purple
Gold
White

Cool Duck and Lots of Hats

Catch It, Jess! and Cat Nap

The Space Race

Pirates Don't Drive Diggers

A Right Royal Mess

To view the whole Maverick Readers scheme, visit our website at
www.maverickearlyreaders.com

Or scan the QR code above to view our scheme instantly!

Quiz Answers: 1a, 2c, 3b, 4c, 5b